The rhythms and cycles of this wonderful world we live in are reflected
and echoed in our own selves and in those whom we love.
I dedicate this story to my wife, Linda, for her bravery and her sea-soul.

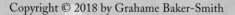

First U.S. edition 2019

Library of Congress Catalog Card Number 2018963124
ISBN 978-1-5362-0575-6

19 20 21 22 23 24 TLF 10 9 8 7 6 5 4 3 2 1

Printed in Dongguan, Guangdong, China

This book was typeset in Adobe Caslon and Bodoni 72.
The illustrations were created digitally.

TEMPLAR BOOKS

an imprint of
Candlewick Press
99 Dover Street
Somerville, Massachusetts 02144
www.candlewick.com

The
Rhythm
of the
Rain

Grahame Baker-Smith

templar books
an imprint of Candlewick Press

Issac was playing in his favorite pool
on the side of the mountain.
He felt spots of rain on his cheek and looked up.
The clouds above him were turning dark.

He emptied his jar of water into the pool as the rain made
little streams that ran out of it. When the rain stopped,
Issac raced the streams down the mountainside.

He followed them to the river that
ran past his home and then plunged down a waterfall.

*Somewhere in all that tumbling is the water
from my little jar*, Issac thought.

As the river went on, it got deeper and wider.
Creatures came out of the woods to drink and to wash,
and fish leaped high out of the swelling water.

On and on the river flowed,
winding through the country . . .

and winding through the city.
And everywhere it went, people and
creatures found a use for it.

Eventually it joined the great ocean.

Where is the water from my jar now? Issac wondered.

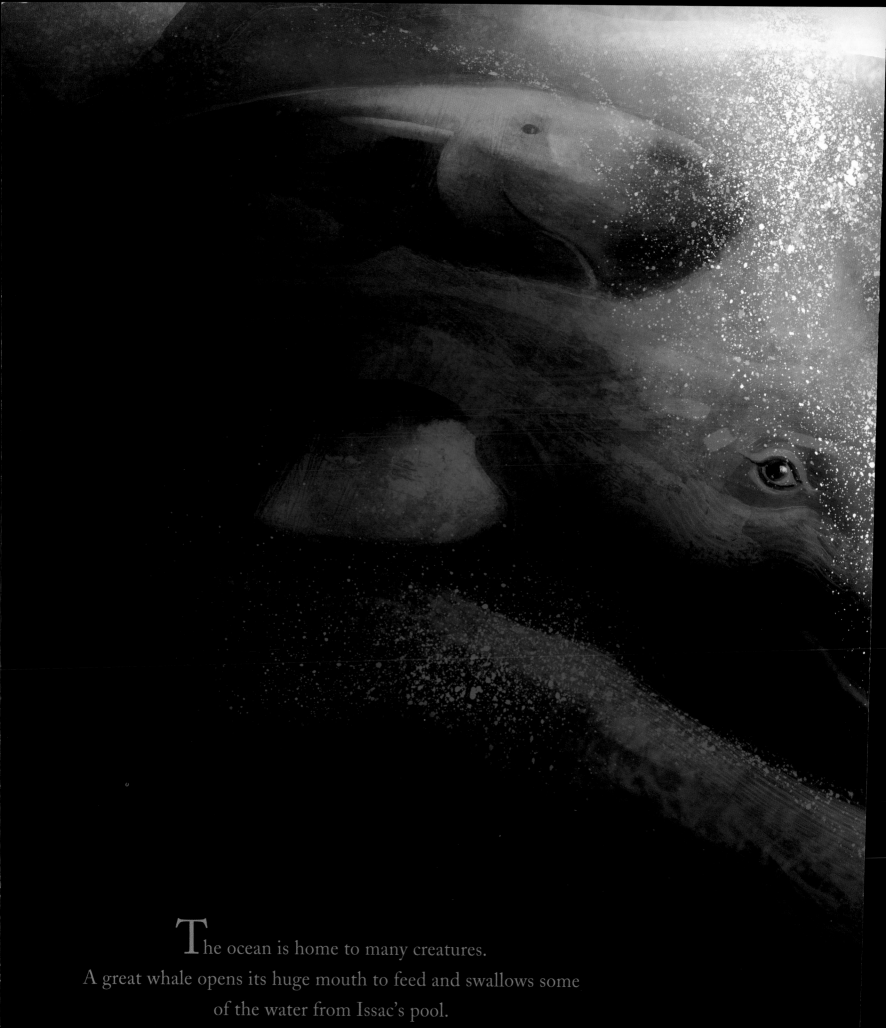

The ocean is home to many creatures.
A great whale opens its huge mouth to feed and swallows some
of the water from Issac's pool.

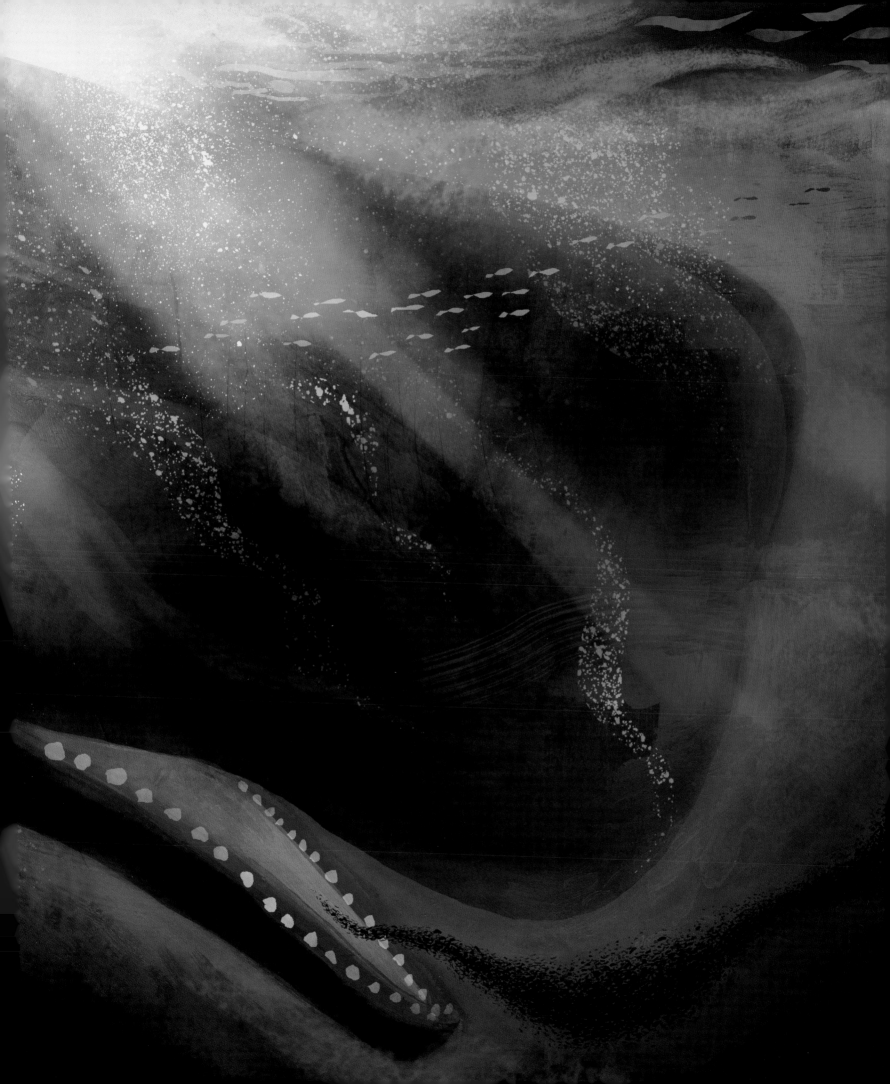

Later, by the light of the moon, the whale rises and blows a great fountain into the starry night. The water falls like rain back into the sea.

It flows with the currents that run like rivers, deep, deep
down, where the sun's light never shines.

Then it rises to ride a storm all night long.

In the calm morning, the sun turns the waves golden.
The ocean steams in the heat, and some of its water climbs, as mist, into the sky.
The mist cools and gathers into a cloud that floats over a mountain
in a country far, far away from Issac's pool.

The clouds release their gift of water.
They fill the pool where a little girl is playing.

Down the mountain the river runs.
Elephants and giraffes, flamingos and zebras
celebrate the return of the rain.

On and on the water runs . . .

back to the sea . . .

where a giant squid,
surprised by a shark . . .

creates a cloud of ink,
sucks in some seawater,
and jets away to safety.

Once more the sun heats the ocean,
and some of the seawater rises as steam
into the sky,
where it forms into clouds.
And then rain falls on the land as it has
done for millions of years.

Then thirsty flowers draw the
wandering water into themselves,
waving like bright flags around
the pool where Issac plays.